HIS GRANDFATHER'S WATCH

N.R. WALKER

COPYRIGHT

Cover Artist: Sara York
His Grandfather's Watch © 2015 N.R. Walker
Second Edition

All Rights Reserved:

Warning

Intended for an 18+ audience only. This book contains material that maybe offensive to some and is intended for a mature, adult audience. It contains graphic language, explicit sexual content, and adult situations.

Trademarks:

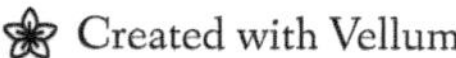 Created with Vellum

His Grandfather's Watch

N.R. Walker

CHAPTER ONE

SITTING in the back room at my desk, with a dismantled 1901 Newman's clock, I heard the bell that chimed every time a customer walked through the door. My dad was behind the counter, and I heard him greet the customer, making small talk, discussing whatever antique it was they'd brought with them.

It's what we did.

My father's love of all things antique grew into this business, Harper's Antiquities. Dad was the expert and Mom did the research, but they both traveled, scouring the globe for their life's passion. My brother Scott did antique furniture restoration, but it wasn't something I ever saw myself doing. Then I started helping out when I was a kid at school, and I found a love of clocks.

It's my specialty.

I could hear Dad talking to the customer, but didn't pay them any mind until I heard my name.

"Alex?"

Putting down the part in my hand, I walked through to the showroom where I found my father and the customer he was talking to. Very different from my pale skin, black hair and grayish eyes, he was a good looking guy, similar age to me, but with sandy brown, kinda longish hair, tanned skin and blue eyes. He was holding a pocket watch in his hand.

"This is my son, Alex," Dad explained. "He's the expert on watches like yours."

I extended my hand in professional courtesy. "Hello."

"Callum Winters," he said by way of greeting, putting the watch on the counter before shaking my hand. There was an accent, Southern I thought, but I wasn't sure.

Dad waited for us to let go of each other's hands, then he looked at me and smiled. "Callum was just telling me he'd like to know more about this watch."

I looked at the silver watch casing and fob chain, then at its owner. I reached my hand toward the watch, but before I touched it, I asked, "May I?"

"Sure," he nodded.

Picking it up, I could tell a few things from a visual inspection. "This casing was a popular design in the 1940's," I told him. Gently, I opened the casing to reveal the quartz face. "The dial is Hamilton, but I won't know dates or maker for certain, unless I take the back off and look at the movement."

"Could you do that?" he asked. His accent was definitely southern. "I was hoping to know as much about it as I could."

I smiled. "Sure. I'll need to grab some details, and I should be able to look at it in about two days. Then I can tell you everything I know."

Callum nodded. "That'd be great." We looked at each other for a little too long, and I couldn't help but wonder if this cute, Southern man was gay.

Dad seemed to think so, because with a cheeky smirk,

he handed me the register log, looked between us and not-so subtly said, "Callum, I'll leave you in Alex's very capable hands." He pointed behind us, "I have... *stuff*... I need to do out the back."

Callum politely thanked him, and I considered kicking my father in the shins. We were behind the counter, so it's not like Callum would have seen me do it. But Dad must have picked up on the look I gave him, because he smiled, turned quickly and disappeared through the door.

I grabbed a pen, handed Callum the register and asked him to fill in his details. I picked up the watch, turning it over in my hands. It was a nice piece, and I couldn't help but ask, "What do you know about the watch?"

He looked up from the paperwork. "Um, it was my grandfather's. That's about all I know."

He handed me the completed form, and I told him as procedure, I required some ID. Taking out his wallet, he handed me his driver's license. His Texas driver's license.

"I just moved here," he said. "I've got my change of address receipt here somewhere."

He started looking through his wallet, and I stopped him. "No, its fine. I just need to sight photo ID, that's all."

He smiled kindly and nodded. "So, two days?"

"Yeah. I'm half way through another job. Then I can look at this, and I'll give you a call when I'm done," I told him. "Is there anything in particular you're looking for?"

He shrugged one shoulder and shook his head. "No, not really. Just dates, make, model... to be honest, I'm not really sure."

As I was putting the watch and paperwork in a paper envelope, I asked him, "Would you like a valuation?"

"No," he said simply. "Monetary value isn't important."

He thanked me, I told him I'd be in touch and he left.

When I walked back into the workshop, Dad grinned at me. "He was a *nice* young man," he said.

"Mom!" I yelled to the upstairs office, where my mother would have undoubtedly had her head in a catalogue. "Dad's trying to set me up again."

She yelled back, "Was he cute?"

Oh for crying out loud.

He was actually, but that's not the point. Dad chuckled at me.

Ignoring him, I sat the pocket watch on my desk and turned my attention back to the clock I was working on.

I managed to ignore both my parents and their comments about cute, brown-haired watch owners until they got bored and left me alone. And I managed to push the thoughts of the pocket watch and its handsome Texan owner out of my mind until it was time to go home.

I ARRIVED BACK at work a little before nine in the morning and headed straight for my desk, which was more like a workstation, when the paper sleeve holding the pocket watch caught my eye.

I picked it up and took the watch out, feeling the cool, heavy weight of it in my hand. I didn't hear my dad come up behind me, and his voice startled me. "How's Mr. Yeo's clock coming along?"

"Oh, shit! You scared me," I said with a laugh, clutching my heart. Then looking back to the clock I had half done, I told him, "Um, it should be ready by lunchtime tomorrow."

He nodded thoughtfully. "I think you should do the watch instead."

I looked at the pocket watch I was still holding. "Why?"

"Because Mr. Yeo is a collector," he replied with a shrug. "To him that clock is just something else he acquired. Even old Mr. Yeo will tell you that. But this," he pointed to the watch in my hand, "this means something."

Dad smiled at me. "Mr. Yeo can wait a day or two. He won't mind. I'll even phone him myself."

"Are you sure?" I asked.

He nodded. "He wants me to go with him to look at an 18th Century hand-carved Italian rococo centre table he'd seen at an auction house anyway, so I need to speak to him."

"Okay," I agreed. Within twenty minutes, I had Mr. Yeo's clock itemized and put away and the silver pocket watch in front of me.

I made my usual notes as I proceeded detailing. There was nothing remarkable about it, until I removed the back casing.

Because what I found hidden in the back of the pocket watch was unlike anything I'd encountered before.

I took out the client form with Callum Winters' details on it and picked up the phone. "Callum Winters? It's Alex, from Harper Antiquities. I'm calling about your watch."

"Yes?" he answered, unsure.

"Can you come into the store?" I asked. "There's something you need to see."

WHEN CALLUM ARRIVED, I led him through to the workshop and offered him a seat at my desk. I'd never had a customer back here; I guess there'd never been a reason to.

Until then.Until him.

He looked at my desk, which had his grandfather's

pocket watch pulled into three pieces. "What is it?" he asked.

"When I took the casing off, I found this," I told him, pointing to the small square of yellowed paper.

"A photograph?"

I nodded. "And an inscription engraved into the back of the watch."

Callum blinked, absorbing the information, before he picked up the photo. It was small, only an inch and a half square, black and white and aged, but there was no mistaking who or what the picture was of.

Two men, about 18 years old, dressed in outfits from possibly the 1940's. But that's not what was remarkable about it. It's how they were standing. They were facing the camera with an arm each around the other; not in a brotherly love embrace, but an embrace that shows a history – an *intimate* history.

They were lovers.

Callum stared at the photo for quite some time before he asked, "What's the inscription?"

I showed him the watch, and I stared at him as he read it.

H. So I am with you, always. Forever yours, B.

"Do you know who they are?" I asked.

"Um..." Callum stalled. Then looking back at the photograph, he said, "I think that's my grandfather. The man with blond hair, though he's very young."

"And the other man?"

Callum shook his head no. "I've not seen him before." He looked at the two men for a long moment. "They look... um, like they're..."

"A happy couple," I finished for him. He looked at me,

then *really* looked at me. There was a brief moment of understanding between us, from one gay man to another.

He gave me a small nod and half a smile before looking back at the photograph in his hand. "Yes, they do, don't they?"

I cleared my throat and brought the subject back to the pocket watch. "Do you know who the H and B are in the inscription?"

"H would be for my grandfather. His name was Hale," Callum explained. "But I don't know who the B is."

Then my dad spoke. I didn't even know he was there. "Would anyone in your family know?"

Callum looked at my father, then to me and then back at the photograph he was holding. "My parents died last year," he offered quietly. "There's only my grandmother and me."

Oh.

Dad asked, "Maybe she would know?"

Callum shrugged. "She has dementia..." his words trailed off.

"Oh, I see," Dad said softly.

"She's in a care facility now," Callum continued to explain. "But I moved up here to be with her anyway."

I was at a loss as to what to say, so I offered him a sympathetic smile instead.

After a long moment's silence, he asked, "Anything else you can tell me about the watch?"

"It is a 1941 Hamilton Art Deco," I told him. "I have all the particulars written down for you, but I can tell you this much..." he looked directly at me, as I told him, "...whoever it was, this person with the initial B, who gave your grandfather this watch, must have loved him very much."

Callum's eyes widened before he smiled sadly. "How do you know?"

"The casing is fine silver, but the watch is 14 karat white gold. I'd imagine back in 1940 it would have cost a small fortune, considering how scarce commodities were during the war."

He was silent for a while. Then he whispered, to me or to himself, I wasn't sure. "I just wish I knew."

"I hope the photo and the inscription leads to finding out more," I said.

My dad was now standing beside Callum and asked, "You've got no one else that can help you, have you?"

The brown haired man shook his head and spoke quietly. "No, not really. I mean, I could ask my Gramma, but I'm not sure it'd do me any good."

"Is there anything else we can do to help?" I asked, though I wasn't altogether sure why.

"Oh, no," he shook his head. "You've done more than enough. I wasn't even expecting this much. I was worried when you rang. You said two days but called me the next day, I thought something must have gone wrong."

"Oh, heavens no," Dad reassured him. "I told Alex to start on your watch because I could tell it means a lot to you. We didn't mean to worry you."

Callum smiled, but before he could speak, my Dad's eyes lit up. "Alex could go with you!"

My mouth fell open. "He could what?"

"Oh, no," Callum was quick to join in. "I don't expect you to do that." He stood, clearly nervous, and he started to leave.

Dad glared at me, then looked pointedly at Callum. "Alex!" he hissed at me.

Dad was right. No one should have to deal with this alone.

Shit.

"Callum, wait," I said, standing up and walking over to him. "If you want someone to go with you to see your grandmother and ask some questions, then I'll go with you."

Callum looked at me, and his mouth opened and closed, twice.

So I told him, "You can say no, if you'd prefer. It just seems you shouldn't do this on your own, that's all."

He shifted his weight from foot to foot, but he nodded. Quietly, to two complete strangers, he admitted, "It's hard not knowing anyone, not having anyone I can talk to. Gramma has good and bad days, and I know asking her questions will be hit and miss. I don't want to upset her..."

"But you need to know about your grandfather's relationship with this other man, don't you?" I asked.

He nodded. "Maybe it will help me understand... a lot of things." He shrugged. "Or maybe it won't. I don't know."

"Do you want me to go with you?" I asked him again.

He gave me a sad smile. "I'd like that, yeah."

"I'll just grab my things," I said, quickly walking back to my desk.

I risked a glance at my dad, who was standing out of Callum's line of sight. And yes, he was grinning like an idiot. "See you tomorrow," he said.

Tomorrow? What about today? It was barely 10 AM.

"Oh," my father added, waggling his eyebrows. "I'll give you a call later... to see how *things* went..."

I snorted. Yeah, right.

I pocketed my keys and my phone, but handed the photograph and the watch to Callum. "You ready?"

He replied, "As I'll ever be."

CHAPTER TWO

AS WE WERE GETTING into Callum's car to go and see his grandmother, he thanked me again.

"It really is no problem," I reassured him. "I couldn't even imagine going through what you've been through. Not having any family..." I trailed off, realizing it wasn't something he probably wanted to talk about.

His eyes flinched at my mention of his family, but he smiled. "Yeah, your dad seems pretty cool."

I rolled my eyes. "I apologize for him; he's a little... *insistent* sometimes."

Callum chuckled a warm, throaty sound. "Yesterday, when I first came into the shop, I wasn't sure if he was implying anything, or if I was imagining things."

I groaned. "Every time a guy walks in and doesn't have a woman on his arm, my father is trying to set me up."

The words came out so easily. I'd just outed myself to a man, who I didn't know, who I *thought* was gay, without a second thought.

But Callum looked from the road to me, and he grinned.

"So, your parents are pretty cool with you being gay?" he asked, but it wasn't really a question.

I nodded. "Yeah. They were a bit worried for me, when I first came out, but they accept me as I am."

Callum was quiet as he concentrated on driving. After a while he told me, "I never told my parents. You know, before they died... they never knew."

Oh, shit. My voice was kinda quiet, "Did anyone else know?"

"The few guys I've been with sure knew," he said with a smirk, trying to lighten the mood. "But no, no one else. My friends back home... maybe they knew," he shrugged, "but I never said outright that I was gay."

Then he said, "When I decided to come up here to look after Gramma, I decided I wouldn't hide anymore." He looked at me and shrugged again. "I don't have any reason to hide anymore."

And for the remainder of the drive, I learned he'd been here in San Francisco for about eight weeks, he lived two suburbs over from me, and he hadn't seen much of the city, but he'd have liked to.

I also learned he has perfect teeth, his eyes were bluer than the sky out the window behind him, the dimple in his right cheek was more pronounced than the one in his left, and I learned that I *really* liked his accent.

He pulled his car into a parking lot, using a security card to lift the boom gate. Looking around, the place didn't particularly look hospital-like. It was a relatively new, single story complex with large windows and manicured gardens.

It looked expensive.

Callum turned off the ignition but made no move to get out of the car. "If she's not having a good day..."

"It's okay," I told him. "If it's not today, then we can come back another day."

And I realized I would. I'd like to spend more time with him.

He looked at me, almost embarrassed. "You're being very kind."

I smiled at him. "You can buy me a coffee to thank me."

He grinned then. "Deal." He looked over at the building, at the entrance doors. "Come on, let's get this over with."

<hr>

THE CARE FACILITY, as Callum called it, was more like an up-market nursing home. It was a hospice; clinical, but welcoming and pleasant. I guessed the budget had something do with that.

We walked through the foyer and down a hospital-looking corridor. There were rooms on each side, and I purposely didn't look inside them. Callum was obviously familiar with the building, like he'd walked these halls a hundred times.

"It's 10:30," he said. "Gramma will be in the communal lounge." He stopped before we walked through the double doors at the end of the hall. "She might not be very lucid today," he said apologetically. "She wasn't very good yesterday."

I nodded and smiled at him. "Everyone has good and bad days."

His eyebrows lifted, and he nodded. "That's true."

Then he smiled and led the way through the doorway. The room itself was huge; there were tables, chairs, lounges with side tables. I was reminded of being a kid in my grand-parents' home before they passed away.

It was just like that, except bigger. There were even crotchet blankets over the backs of the lounges and pictures of flowers and gardens on the walls. There was an upright piano in the corner and a television on the opposite wall.

There were older people sitting, talking, resting. Some were doing activities at the tables, some were up and walking around. There were large glass doors that opened out to a courtyard, and Callum headed straight for them. "When it's not raining, she likes to sit in the sun," he explained. Then he smiled and added, "You can take a girl out of Texas..."

As we walked through, Callum said, "Hello, Mr. Tyler," to a patient here. And one of the nursing staff called Callum by name, saying hello as he walked through the room to the courtyard. It was very obvious he spent a lot of time here.

Once outside, he headed straight over to a lady who was sitting on a bench seat by herself; just like Callum said, enjoying the San Francisco sun.

Callum sat down next to her. "Hello," he said. Unsure, I presumed, of how he'd be received.

"Hello," she replied back to him.

"Gramma, it's Callum," he said.

"I know," she said. But I could see Callum wasn't convinced.

He smiled sadly. "How are they treating you today?"

"Oh fine, fine," she said with a curt nod, and they made small talk like strangers on a bus.

She was a small, elderly lady I presumed to be in her eighties. Her gray hair was long and swept up in some kind of bun or knot, and her eyes were a faraway blue. It was fairly apparent today was not a good day.

Callum made introductions. "This is Alex. Alex, this is Maria Winters."

She said hello, and I did the same, then she started asking Callum questions about morning tea. He offered to get her a cup of tea, and he nodded for me go with him.

Callum led the way to the visitor's kitchen, but he was quiet. Another nurse walked past and stopped to smile at him. "How is she today?"

He shook his head. "Not so great."

The nurse, an older woman, rubbed his arm, gave him a sympathetic smile and kept on her way. Callum busied himself with making a cup of tea. "She doesn't remember me today."

I wasn't sure what to say to this man who I barely knew. I hoped my presence there with him was enough.

He looked at me and smiled dejectedly, and his voice was quiet. "Sorry to have wasted your time."

"Callum," I touched his arm as I spoke. "It's not a waste of my time. I think what you're doing is great, with your grandmother. Not many people our age would do that."

"She's my only family," he said. He picked up the cup and looked at me and smiled. "And I better get this back to her, or she'll cuss me out."

I smiled and followed him back to the courtyard. He sat with his grandmother, and they discussed inconsequential things. He really was a great guy. He smiled, even though I could see how much it hurt him. He made sure she was comfortable and asked if she needed anything.

And I sat and watched them. I listened and joined in occasionally, but mostly just looked on. Soon enough it was lunchtime and we walked her inside and found her seat. I was told the residents usually have rest time after their midday meal, and I suggested to Callum we find somewhere close by to grab some lunch. "We can come back after she's rested."

Callum couldn't hide his surprise, or his smile. "Are you sure?"

I smiled back at him. "Anyway, you owe me a coffee."

He grinned, and I decided I'd like to see him smile more often.

WE FOUND a café and ordered lunch. Everything with him was all very easy. He thanked me again for coming with him. "I didn't realize how much I missed conversation," he said with a shake of his head. "I feel like I'm talking your ear off."

I smiled with him. "I like having my ears chewed on."

His eyes widened at my words, and I realized how it must have sounded. "I didn't mean it like that," I said quickly, feeling the heat of embarrassment creep over my cheeks.

He laughed then, and his eyes shined. I'm sure he had something to say, but I was thankfully saved by the waitress offering coffee refills.

Then he asked about work; how I got into antiquities, and why clocks?

I told him about my parents' love for relics and history and how the business grew. I explained how when I was real little, there was a cuckoo clock I was fascinated with. "I would set it to keep going off. How I never drove my parents mad, I'll never know. But then the older I got, the real appreciation was for the older clocks."

I'd never really explained this to anyone else. "It amazes me how these instruments of time were made so long ago, some of them hundreds of years. I can only imagine the hands that built them all those years ago..." I felt a bit foolish for saying this out loud, but he nodded for me to continue. "That someone handcrafted a watch, or a clock, and here it is, some hundred years later still counting time like the day it was made. Whenever I see a watch, or a clock, I can't help but wonder who held it in their hands, who looked at it, where it's been..."

Callum smiled at me. He didn't say anything; he just smiled.

I sipped my coffee and asked him what he did for a living. "Nothing right now," he said. "I visit my Gramma every day, but back in Texas I'd left college not long ago."

He saw me counting years in my head, trying to work out his age. He smiled. "I'm 23," he said. "I did four years at college. I studied English Literature, graduated in the Spring." Then he added softly, "My parents died that summer, so I never actually started work..."

"I'm very sorry," I said, such inadequate words.

"Thanks," he shrugged. "Eventually I sorted through belongings, and I found the pocket watch in with my dad's things. There was no mention of it in any insurance records or will documents, but I remember when my grandfather died, my dad saying something about an old pocket watch."

"When did your grandfather pass away?"

"I was about twelve," he answered. "I remember some argument between my dad and my grandmother about the watch. That's *why* I remember it, because they argued. I wouldn't have remembered it otherwise. I remember my dad yelling, *'It's just a watch.'* I'd not given it another thought, until I found it in his safe."

"I never expected to uncover a photograph," he sighed. "Or what the photo would mean..." his words trailed away. Then we were both quiet for a while.

He sighed again. "I don't know if Gramma will even be

able to tell me anything about the watch or the photograph, or if it will just upset her" he said. "But I want to know as much about the watch as I can... to see if there was any obvious reason why it would have been a bone of contention between them."

He stared at his coffee. "She's easily upset. She asked me once, when I told her I was Callum, where my parents were." He turned the cup in his hand and looked at it when he spoke. "I told her there had been a car accident and they'd died. She cried and cried – I broke her heart." He looked at me then, and said, "Then two hours later, she asked me where they were again."

"Oh, Callum," I breathed his name. I shook my head. I didn't know what else to say.

"It's hard when she calls me Peter," he said. "That's my dad. She calls me that more than she calls me Callum." He finished his coffee, took a deep breath and shook his head. "I must sound like a basket case," he said with a chuckle. He looked at me, and his smile faded. "But I really appreciate you being here today."

I slipped my hand over his and squeezed it. "I'm glad I'm here." I pulled my hand away to look at my watch. "Should we head back?"

Callum seemed surprised by the time. He nodded, "I didn't realize how long we'd been here."

Truthfully, neither had I. It was almost three; we'd been chatting for over two and a half hours.

He paid the tab, citing it was his thanks, and we headed back to see his Gramma.

CHAPTER THREE

AS WE WALKED IN, Callum told me his grandmother's usually more lucid after resting. And when we saw her, she did seem more alert. She was in her room this time. It was private and surprisingly, quite nice. She had her bed, an ensuite, a small table and a dresser.

She stood when we walked in and kissed Callum on the cheek. "Oh, I knew you'd be visiting me today," she said.

Then she eyed me and clicked her tongue. "Peter dear, don't be rude. Introduce your friend."

Callum's face fell at the mention of his father's name. He tried to smile. "This is Alex. Alex this is Maria Winters."

We exchanged pleasantries, though she eyed me cautiously. I was well over a foot taller than her; she was tiny compared to us standing men, so I asked her if I could please sit down, hoping she'd feel more comfortable if I wasn't towering over her.

She seemed pleased I asked permission to sit, and she smiled at me. "Can I get you boys anything?"

"No Gram-" Callum stopped himself just short of

calling her his name for her. Instead, he finished with, "We're fine."

Callum took a deep breath and said, "Can I show you something?"

"Yes, dear," she replied pleasantly.

He took the watch out of his pocket and held it in his hand for her to see.

Mrs. Winters' eyes darted to the watch, and they widened when she realized what it was. She definitely recognized it.

"Where did you get that?" she asked, rather coolly.

"I found it," he answered. It was a little white lie, but it wasn't like he could her tell the truth. He couldn't exactly say it's rightfully his now that both her husband and son had died.

She shook her head no. "It should have been buried with him."

Callum leaned back in the chair, like her words weighed too much. "Why?"

"Hale wanted it buried with him," she said with hard eyes. "But you wanted it, right or wrong. I told you it wasn't an heirloom, Peter; it wasn't to be kept."

Callum's face twisted. So that's what the argument had been about. Callum's father had disputed *his* father's dying wish and kept the watch.

It's just a watch.

Except it was never just a watch to Hale. It was a token of love, a forbidden love perhaps. His lover had given it to him.

Callum's voice was quiet. "Whose name started with B?"

His grandmother was silent for a moment. "No one, why?"

"Do you know who the watch is from?"

She didn't answer, and I saw she was tiring quickly. "I might rest now," she said quietly, standing up, only to walk to her bed to lay down.

"My brother William was such a kind soul," she went on to say, seemingly talking to herself. "War is such a horrid, horrid waste."

And it seemed all sensible conversation was, at least for the moment, over.

"It sure is, Gramma," Callum answered mechanically. Then he asked her, "Can I get you anything?"

She told him to stop fussing, and he smiled, but his heart wasn't in it.

"William was a bliss boy," Mrs. Winters whispered, and her eyes hada faraway look in them. If she was remembering or reliving it, I wasn't sure. Then she mumbled something I couldn't make out; she was exhausted.

Callum sat beside her bed and held her hand. "It's okay," he said. "You rest now. I'll be back tomorrow."

"You're a sweet boy," she replied, tapping his hand. "And Peter, bring Charlotte with you next time. She's such a nice girl."

Callum didn't answer for a second, and I realized a little too late, it wasn't that he *wouldn't* answer, it was that he *couldn't* answer. It dawned on me then, Charlotte must be his mom. He sucked back a shaky breath and finally answered with, "Sure."

Callum walked out first, and I followed him. I could tell he was trying to compose himself, trying to hold it together. He didn't say a word, and when we got to the car, I stopped him.

"I'm sorry," he said. He looked away and exhaled loudly. "It just gets me when she mentions her."

"Is Charlotte your mom?"

His eyes filled with water, and he nodded.

Oh, fuck.

Oh, Callum.

I did the only thing that felt right, the only thing one person could do in this situation, I stepped right up to him and put my arms around him. At first I think I shocked him, but he soon relaxed into me, and his tears began to fall.

This poor man. The word *alone* didn't begin to describe how he must have felt. I couldn't even begin to fathom it... He'd lost his parents, moved away from his friends to be closer to his grandmother – his only living relative – and she didn't even recognize him.

I held him tightly, rubbing my hands over his back. I could feel his face buried into my neck, his hands fisted into my shirt, and I just held him. I knew from experience when things weren't great, there was something about the human connection of being hugged.

It had healing properties.

He slowly pulled away and wiped at his face and nose. "I'm sorry," he said, embarrassed. "I'm sorry."

"It's okay," I told him. "You're dealing with a lot, Callum. Don't apologize."

He scrubbed his hands across his face and shook his head, trying to make sense of what his grandmother just told him. "I don't know what to believe. Why would my father want to keep the watch against his own father's wishes? If he wanted it to be buried with him, why dispute that?"

"Maybe your dad wanted to keep any part of his father with him for as long as he could..."

Callum looked at me then, and I could see it was a concept he truly understood. He nodded. He leaned against his car, ran his hands over his face and through his hair, and sighed. "What a mess."

"You didn't show her the photo?" I said, though it's more of a statement than a question.

He shook his head. "I couldn't."

"Yeah, I know," I answered softly. I saw how hard it was for him in there. Maybe he needed some fresh air. "Wanna go for a walk?" I suggested.

He smiled weakly and gave me a nod. "There's a park up the block," he said, giving a pointed glance up the street. "I sit there sometimes while Gramma's resting."

He was right. It was only a short walk, and it was peaceful. I could see why he'd want to sit there and collect his thoughts. We found a bench seat and settled into small talk. He looked so damn tired; a bone deep weariness. He'd endured so much for someone so young. It was evident in his eyes; sad and sorrowful, but strong and resilient.

We sat there in the shade of the trees and talked for the better part of an hour. His tears were long dried up, and the puffiness from his eyes was gone. We talked of movies and music and how he hoped to one day put his time at college to productive use.

I asked him what he wanted to do with his life.

"I want to write," he answered. "I have half a dozen, half-written things I've started, but when my parents died, everything just got put on hold. Then I moved here." Then he added, almost as an afterthought, "My life hasn't been about me in a long time."

I leaned in and squeezed his hand. "Then you should write."

And then like a wrecking ball through this quiet, heartfelt moment, my cell phone rang. I grimaced apologetically, and pulled my phone from my pocket. I checked caller ID and groaned. "It's my brother."

I flipped my phone open, and there were no pleasantries, no greetings. "We still on for tonight?" he asked loud enough for Callum to hear.

"Yeah, not bad.Yourself?" I asked sarcastically.

He ignored me completely. "Well, are you comin' or not? I need to book a table."

I looked at Callum. And I was torn. I wasn't ready to say goodbye to him just yet. "Hang on," I told my brother, covered the phone and looked at Callum. "Dinner and drinks with the guys. Want to come?"

His eyes went wide, so I rephrased the question. "Would you like to have dinner with me tonight?"

He gave me a still surprised, but shy smile and a bit of nod. I took it as a yes.

I smiled at him, lifted the phone back to my ear. "Scott? Two seats, please."

And there was only silence on the other end of the phone. "Scott? You there?"

"Uh, yeah..." he answered, unsure. "Um, are you bringing a *date?*"

"Scott," I warned, but it was too late.

He crowed, "Ohmyfuckinggod! Alex's got a date!" I'm pretty sure he just announced it to a three block radius.

Knowing Callum just heard that entire conversation, I rolled my eyes and flipped the phone closed. "That would be my brother."

He smiled, but looked a little unsure.

Closing the distance between us, I put a reassuring hand on his arm. "It's just a few guys, dinner, a beer or two and some laughs, that's all. We don't have to stay late," I told him. He still looked unsure, or nervous even. "When was the last time you had a night out?"

"A while ago," he admitted quietly.

"Then it's settled."

"Where exactly are we going?" he asked.

"Renata's Bar and Grill," I told him. "Best steak and ribs outside of Texas, apparently."

Callum smiled. "I'll be the judge of that."

It was good to see him smile. I grinned at him. Then he turned serious and asked, "Is he... does he mind... you know...?"

"That I'm gay?" I asked.

His eyes widened again, but he nodded.

"He couldn't care less," I told him. "All the guys who will be there tonight know. Out of the six of us that usually meet up to watch the Friday night game, two of us are gay. We've known each other for years."

"Oh," he answered softly.

And I forgot this is all so very new to him. So I asked him, "Have you ever gone out in public with a guy before?"

He shook his head. "Not really, no," he admitted quietly. "College was different, but not out on like a date, no."

A date.

I smiled. "Well, tonight shall be your first." Then I quickly added, "Date, first official *date.*"

He looked to the ground all shy-like, but he smiled.

I looked at my watch. "Come on," I said as I stood. "We'd better get going." I couldn't help but smile. I liked Callum. He was a nice guy and I was looking forward to spending more time with him. I mean, it was wonderful he was being so considerate for his grandmother; it said so much about what kind of man he was. And I'd already decided to help him find out what he can about his grandfather.

But maybe, just maybe, I could help him be a twenty three year old too.

CHAPTER FOUR

WE CALLED past my place to freshen up before we went out, because it was closer. I threw my mail on the table and gave him a quick tour of my apartment – not that there was much to see. Callum asked if he was dressed okay for dinner. I looked down at my jeans and tee shirt. "I'm not getting changed," I told him.

I looked him over. He was wearing dark jeans and a light gray button down shirt. "You look great," I said without thinking. So I tried to cover up with, "I mean, over-dressed, if anything."

His eyes widened, and he blushed.

"No, I didn't mean you're wearing too many clothes..." I amended quickly. I felt my own embarrassment heat my cheeks. I took a deep breath and started again. "What I meant to say was what you're wearing is fine."

He smiled shyly. "Thanks."

He excused himself to use the bathroom, and I took some deep breaths trying to get my shit together. Soon enough, we were walking through the front door of Renata's. It was a lively place, almost like a sports bar with fancy saloon-like tables and booths, neon beer signs and huge flat-screens for watching sports.

It was Scott's favorite place.

He was already there, grinning like the Cheshire Cat. I groaned inwardly as we took a seat at the booth, and I made introductions. "Cal, Sam, Alistair, Brian; this is Callum. Callum, this is my brother, Scott."

I gave Scott the be-nice-or-I'll-kill-you stare, and he just grinned, shaking Callum's hand. There were knowing smiles around the table and suggestive glances. Callum just smiled nervously, but he sat closer to me, wiping his hands on his thighs. He was really anxious, so I laid my hand on his leg next to me, silently telling him it was okay.

Then the waitress brought out plates of wings and bread, we ordered drinks and conversations started like any other Friday night. We talked utter crap and laughed through dinner, and I watched Callum smile and chuckle, shaking his head at the guys.

Scott paid out on him because the Dallas Cowboys lost to the San Francisco 49'ers. Callum just laughed it off, telling him the Cowboys let the 49'ers win because Texan men don't like to see girls cry.

Everyone laughed, and Scott grinned. "Yeah, I'll pay that." My brother looked at me with an approving smirk.

When the game started, the others were mesmerized by it; whereas Callum and I just talked between ourselves.

"Your friends are great," he told me with a smile.

"They like you."

He gave me a sad kind of smile. "I take it by the way they look at you, you don't bring tag-alongs very often?"

"Tag-alongs?" I asked with a snort. "If you mean dates, then that'd be a no. I don't go out much. Usually just here with the guys."

He looked at me, so I explained. "I've had... my share of... *dates*," I told him, trying to put it gently. "But I'm not the clubbing type."

He smiled. "Me either."

"Would you like to come here again next Friday night?" I asked, unable to keep the hopeful tone from my voice.

He nodded and grinned. "I'd like that."

Before I could say anything else, Scott slid in across from us. It must have been half time. "So, Callum," he started. "Seeing my brother, huh?"

I groaned. "Scott."

Callum blushed.

"You like men who play with their clocks, huh?"

"Scott," I hissed.

He grinned, all teeth, still looking at Callum. "So... have you seen his *pendulum* yet?"

Callum looked at me and chuckled, a mixture of amused and embarrassed.

I kicked my brother under the table. "How long did it take you to think of that joke, idiot?"

"A while," he admitted. "I have more!"

"Go away," I told him.

Thankfully he got the hint, and when he'd finally left us alone, I apologized for my oaf of a brother. Callum looked at me and smiled. "It's fine, really. He's funny."

I rolled my eyes. "He's embarrassing."

Callum smiled again, but he fought a yawn as he did. He'd had an emotionally charged day, all things considered. So I suggested we leave. We said goodbye to the guys, and I offered to call myself a cab, but Callum was having none of it. He insisted on driving me home, which is why fifteen minutes later, we were sitting in his car in front of my apartment.

He told me it was the best night he'd had in forever.

I couldn't help but smile. Then he yawned again and apologized for it. "It's not the company, believe me. I just don't sleep very well," he said in explanation.

"You should go," I told him. "It's late."

He nodded, then looked at me. "Alex, thank you. For everything."

"It was my pleasure." I opened the car door but turned to look at him. "Can I see you tomorrow?"

He smiled and gave me a nod. "I'll see my Gramma in the morning, but I can come by your place after."

"Oh, I'll be at the shop," I told him. "Saturday mornings are busy, but we close at lunchtime."

"Okay," he said with a smile.

"Okay," I agreed.

I didn't want to say goodbye. I didn't want to leave him just yet, but I knew I couldn't invite him inside either. It was too soon. But figuring a kiss on the cheek wasn't being too forward, I leaned in to kiss him. His eyes widened, and he gasped softly in my ear. I pressed my lips to his cheek, and whispered, "Thank you."

I pulled back just a fraction, and his intense eyes and flushed cheeks almost stole my breath. I couldn't seem to move in either direction; I didn't want to pull away, but didn't want to just launch myself at him either.

But then he nodded, giving me permission to not pull away.

So I kissed him. I pressed my lips to his chastely, sweetly. I moved my lips against his, but didn't move to deepen the kiss. Leaning over the center console never makes for great first kisses, and regardless of how much I wanted to really kiss him properly, I didn't.

I pulled away, only to quickly peck his lips again. "Thank you," I said, smiling.

He grinned, so bashful. It was sort of adorable. I couldn't help but chuckle, making him blush and laugh breathily. "I'll see you tomorrow," I told him, and he nodded quickly.

I got out of the car and walked inside, smiling the entire time.

I WAS STILL SMILING at work the next morning just thinking about his lips, his smile, his dimples. Both Mom and Dad asked me about my day yesterday. I explained briefly what happened, and they nodded thoughtfully as I relayed the story of Callum's grandparents and then his parents.

"So sad," Mom said wistfully.

"So," Dad hedged. "Seeing him again?"

Mom pretended to chastise him, but then she turned to face me, wide-eyed, waiting for me to answer. "Well, are you?"

I rolled my eyes and ignored them, turning back to my work. "I have to get this clock finished by lunchtime," I told them. And then, because the gods of humility must hate me, Scott walked in.

"So, how does Callum like his breakfast?" he asked, loudly, suggestively.

Mom and Dad both gasped in unison and turned to look at me.

"Oh, for the love of... Jesus, Scott. Now they won't ever leave me alone," I huffed at him. "And for your information,"

I looked pointedly at all three of them, "he dropped me off at home. He didn't stay."

Scott batted his eyelids dramatically. "Did you get a goodnight kiss?"

I rolled my eyes and huffed. But then I blushed, giving myself away.

"You did!" Mom squealed.

Oh, shoot me now.

"Go away," I told them, turning back to my table. "*Some* of us have work to do." I figured if I ignored them they'd leave me alone.

Mom and Dad eventually gave up pestering me for any more details and pestered Scott until he got sick of them and left. But it didn't matter, because an hour earlier than expected, Dad, who was then manning the showroom, came grinning into the back room.

"Look who's here!" he said, dragging Callum in with him. Callum smiled when he saw me.

I couldn't explain it considering I'd only known him for such a short time, and I'd only left him about twelve hours ago, but God, it was good to see him. I couldn't help but smile. "You're early."

He nodded, a little embarrassed, I think. "Yeah, I hope you don't mind."

"No, its fine," I told him. Then I looked at my father. He was looking between us like he was watching a tennis match, grinning like Scott. "Dad, you're going to do yourself an injury."

Dad shrugged, and Callum chuckled. I told him, "I'll be about half an hour. I'm almost done."

"Ooh," Dad interrupted, looking excitedly at Callum. "Do you play chess? I just got a Jaques Staunton ebony and boxwood set."

"Um, sure?" Callum answered, looking to me for some kind of reassurance.

I smiled at him. "I won't be much longer." I gave Dad my best *please behave* glare, and he just kept grinning.

Callum and Dad went back out to the front of the shop, giving me time to finish up. I could hear them talking, about what I wasn't sure I wanted to know, but I was pretty sure it has little do with chess. I was just about done when Mom came downstairs. "Who's your father talking to?"

"Callum."

Her eyes widened with excitement, and she smiled as she quickly walked to the door to the showroom. I went with her, thinking it was probably time I saved him anyway. We walked in, and standing behind the counter, we watched as Dad and Callum studied the chessboard in front of them.

"Mmm," Mom hummed. "I can see why you like him. He's cute."

Oh dear God.

I looked at her disbelievingly and spoke to her slowly, "You are aware he can hear you?" We were standing in the same room, ten feet from him for God's sake.

Hearing every word, Callum looked at me, then at my Mom. His cheeks tinted, and he smiled. I made introductions, but before Mom or Dad could do, or say, anything else that would embarrass either of us, I told Dad Mr. Yeo's clock was done and rudely pushed Callum out the door with me.

I exhaled in relief as we walked outside, and he laughed.

"I can see where Scott gets it from. Your parents are... funny."

"Oh, you have no idea..." I mumbled, and he chuckled again.

Before we got to his car, I asked him how his Gramma was.

He answered, "She wasn't too well this morning. She was very tired. She normally naps most of the day when she's like that, so I told the staff I might not be back in this afternoon."

"Did you show her the photograph?"

He shook his head. "No."

I gave him a reassuring smile. "Maybe next time, yeah?"

He nodded and shrugged, but he was hardly convinced. "Are you sure you don't mind coming with me to see her?"

I enjoyed spending time with him. I wanted to get to know him, and I didn't think it was fair he had to deal with this on his own. "I don't mind at all," I told him.

We were standing at his car by then, and I couldn't help but think about something his grandmother said yesterday, how she mentioned her brother. "Do you know much about your Gramma's family? She mentioned her brother..."

Callum looked at me with questioning eyes and shook his head. "No, not really. Why?"

With a shrug, I tried to explain. "I don't know if it was a cognitive leap, but when she was remembering the watch and your grandfather, her mind made a connection to her brother."

He looked at me, and his lips twisted thoughtfully. "I think I have some boxes of old photographs and newspaper clippings at home," he told me. "I could look through them."

"I could help," I offered. His eyes widened in surprise, so I added, "Only if you want me to. I don't want to intrude."

"I'd like that." He smiled. "But first, let's get some lunch."

CHAPTER FIVE

FORTY-FIVE MINUTES LATER, with our lunch in hand, Callum pulled into the security parking of his apartment complex. It was a nice building in a nice neighborhood, and from the car he drove and the clothes he wore, I assumed Callum had some money.

But then it occurred to me, as the sole beneficiary of his parents' estate, it was probably money he'd prefer not to have. He'd have much preferred to have his parents than their money.

We took the stairs, and he opened the door to number fourteen. It was a big place, about twice the size of my place, large tiled floor, mostly whites and creams, except for a dark chocolate colored leather lounge.

I pulled off my shoes and left them inside the door when I was greeted, or inspected rather, by a member of the feline police. A very fluffy cat with a very flat face and an air of self importance gave me the once over, before graciously granting me permission to enter.

"Hey," Callum scooped the cat up affectionately. "Alex,

this is Lucy. Lucy, this is Alex." He then looked at the cat, "You be nice to him."

I laughed, and he shook his head. "She thinks the apartment's hers," he said with a smile. "And I'm just here to serve her."

I chuckled. "I kind of get that impression, yeah."

"She belonged to my mom," Callum said quietly. "Mom spoiled her rotten, and now she expects it." He gave the cat a quick pat and gently put her down.

"I'll just grab these boxes. They're all stacked away," he said, walking into the open lounge area. He waved his hand toward the kitchen. "Kitchen's through there; grab some plates, drinks. Make yourself at home. I'll just be five..." And with that, he disappeared down the hall.

I headed toward the large, stylish kitchen, put our sandwiches on the counter and opened the fridge door. He kept a well-stocked fridge compared to mine, but I decided on two bottles of water, put them on the kitchen counter and walked back out to the lounge room.

There were photo frames, which I probably shouldn't have looked at, but I did. There was an older couple in one of them undoubtedly his parents, because the man was a fifty year old version of Callum.

It was no wonder his grandmother believed it was her son when Callum walked in. They looked so much alike.

There were other photos: Callum in a group of six people, all laughing; Callum in a graduation gown with his arms around his parents. They were all smiling for the camera, oblivious to what the future held for them.

One thing was for certain, Callum had a beautiful smile. Not his small smile I'd already seen, but his uninhibited smile. It was an eye crinkling, double dimpled, perfect teeth kind of smile.

I'd loved to see him smile like that in person.

I didn't hear him come up beside me. "That's my mom and dad on their 25th wedding anniversary," he said quietly. "Me, on graduation day and me and the guys at the lake for spring break."

I'd been caught snooping,there was no point in denying it. So I stated the obvious, "You look like your dad." He nodded and smiled sadly. Then I spoke without thinking. "You have a great smile."

He looked at me, clearly as shocked at my words as I was. I coughed, and he blushed. And I'd just successfully managed to embarrass us both.

I noticed then he was holding not one, but two archive boxes. Needing to divert attention away from me and my stupid mouth, I asked, "You found what you're after?"

He nodded. "Yeah, I think so." He walked over and placed the box on the dining table. "Most of Gramma's things went into storage when she went into the home, but I kept the photo albums. I have some of Mom and Dad's mementos here too..." his words faded away.

He opened the box, putting the lid aside. "I remember my dad talking about some aunts and uncles, but no William."

"Well, let's see what we can find," I said. So we started sorting through the most personal effects of Callum's family while we ate our lunch. There were photo albums, folders of papers and documents; I thought it would be like a family tree search, but instead I just felt like I was invading his privacy terribly.

Time passed in an amicable silence as we gathered pieces of information. I skimmed over words, looking for the name William or Maria, not reading details of things that were not my business. Callum was quiet as he flipped through family photos, sometimes smiling, sometimes not. After a while, I picked up my lot and moved to the lounge. Lucy the cat soon declared me a useful human, because no sooner had I sat down, she was in my lap.

Callum's mouth fell open. "That traitor!" he said with a smile.

I smiled back at him. "I think she likes me."

Callum shook his head at me and put the papers in his hand down on the table. He stretched, ironing out the kinks in his shoulders and headed toward the kitchen. "Want a drink?"

He opened the fridge and started to call out drink options, but I couldn't concentrate on what he was saying because a yellowed square of dated newspaper caught my eye.

"Callum!"

"Yeah, what is it?" he walked out from the kitchen and looked at me.

"You said your Gramma's maiden name was James?" I asked, and he nodded. "Look at this," I said, excitedly. "I think I found something."

I started reading. "'12th November 1942. Local boy, William James, known to his friends as Billy, was killed in action...'"

Callum looked at me with wide blue eyes and sat down beside me. His voice was quiet, "Billy. The B is for Billy."

I nodded. "I think so."

"My grandmother's brother?" he said, thinking aloud. "Billy gave Hale the watch... Billy was in love with the man who would become my grandfather."

I nodded. "From the photo of the two of them together, I'd say your grandfather was in love with Billy, too."

He blinked and swallowed loudly. I handed Callum the

newspaper clipping so he could read it for himself. He then told me, "The article goes on to say 'William James, eighteen years old, had been in the First Armored Division of the Fort Bliss...'" He stopped mid-sentence and looked at me. "Gramma called him a Bliss Boy. I didn't know what she was talking about."

I thought she was talking nonsense too, not that I'd ever tell Callum that.

I smiled at him. "And now you know."

Callum stared at the newspaper clipping for a long while, reading and rereading it. I stood up, keeping Lucy in my arms, and walked over to the table to get the photo of the two men and the watch.

I sat back down next to Callum and scratched a not-amused-for-being-woken-up Lucy under the ears until I was forgiven. I handed the photo to Callum and looked over the watch for the hundredth time.

Then it was my turn to think out loud. "The inscription says 'So I'll be with you, always'. Maybe Billy gave it to him before he went to war, so he'd always have him with him."

"But he never came back," Callum finished. "And Hale married Maria, the sister of the man he loved."

He looked from me back to the photograph. "It's sad, isn't it? So tragic."

"Yes, it is."

Callum frowned. "I know what it was like growing up in my family in the 21st century," he said quietly, shaking his head. "I can't imagine what it was like for these two back in the '40's. The lengths they must have gone to in order keep their relationship a secret."

"Well, it wasn't a complete secret," I told him.

"What do you mean?"

I nodded pointedly to the photo in his hand. "Someone had to take that picture."

He looked at me, and his wide blue eyes sparked with recognition. "Gramma."

<hr>

AFTER A BIT MORE LOOKING, Callum managed to find a family portrait of the James family. In the photo, Maria, Callum's grandmother is standing next to a tall, black haired boy with a baby face and a kind smile. He's younger in this photo, but there was no mistaking it. It was Billy James in both photographs.

Having packed away the photo albums and files of papers, it had gotten quite late. "I'm going to show Gramma the photograph of Billy and Hale tomorrow," he said.

"She has a church service on Sunday mornings, so I won't go in until she's had her lunch and rested," he explained. "I know chances are it will upset her, but I need to know."

He leaned his head against the back of the sofa and looked at me. "I always felt so... *detached* from my family. Don't get me wrong, I had a great childhood, never wanted for anything. But I always knew I was *different* from them. There was no way I could have sat my parents down and told them I liked guys."

"And this," he went on to say, "this makes me feel a bit closer, ya know? To know I'm like my grandfather... it means a lot."

"I know exactly." I did know. I knew exactly what he meant. "I could go with you again, if you'd like me to."

"Are you sure?" he asked. "You've already done so

much." He sounded unsure, but I could see it in his face that he wanted me to.

"I'd like to go," I told him.

He smiled. "That'd be great, thank you."

As much as I'd enjoyed this time with him, I told him I should go home. He hesitated, nervous. "Um, you could... stay..." then he added quickly, "if you want to?"

My stomach flipped at his offer. I exhaled loudly and smiled. "Uh, Callum if I stay..." oh hell, I wasn't sure how to say this, so I opted for the truth. "I'm not sure I'll be able to control myself."

A deep heat colored his cheeks, and his voice was so quiet I almost didn't hear him. "I wouldn't mind."

My stomach flipped again, and my heart skipped a beat. And then he looked at me with vulnerability and hope in his eyes.

I nodded, and he smiled.

I whispered, "Can I kiss you?"

His eyes widened, darkened. And he nodded.

This time there was no center console between us, no hesitation, no doubt.

I'd spent the last two days with this guy and witnessed some of the most profound family moments of his life. We'd started out strangers, and then there I was, about to press my lips to his.

My fingers traced his jaw as my lips touched his. Warm, soft but firm... masculine. My heart was pounding in my chest. When he moved his lips, I could feel the stubble on his chin and it spurred me to deepen the kiss. I opened his lips with mine, my hand held his jaw and he responded in kind.

He pushed his open mouth against mine, and I gave him my tongue in return. His hands slid around my waist, and he pulled our bodies together, aligning us perfectly as he leaned back on the sofa, pulling me with him. His taut, angular body molded against mine. I could *feel* him. His body, his kiss, his hands on me, his tongue in my mouth set my blood to warm. I tried to curb my desire, I tried to reign it in.

Then he moaned.

And I kissed him harder. Deeper.

I held him tighter. Closer.

With my hands on his hips, I settled over him and pressed myself against him. And I was getting hard. He could feel it; I knew he could. Because I could feel him. And I wanted him. I wanted him under me; I wanted to push myself inside him. I wanted to make him come while I was inside him.

But I wanted more than that.

With him.

I wanted to take my time. I wanted to show him, prove to him he could be happy, and give him that human connection he's been missing.

I wanted to make him happy. I wanted to be the one who made him smile that breath-stealing smile.

What I didn't want, was to rush this, or fuck it up.

I pulled my mouth from his and stilled my hands on his hips. I didn't pull away from him; my forehead leaned against his, and we tried to catch our breaths.

"Jesus." He breathed in raggedly, his lips swollen and wet.

"Mmm," I chuckled and smiled. "Cal, I don't want to stop, but we should." I sat up, pulling him with me. I slid my arms around him and pecked his lips with mine; we were a mass of heaving breaths and tangled legs. I told him, "I want to take this slow. I want to see where it goes. I know it's only early days - hell, it's only been two days - but I think this has potential to be something..."

His eyes shined and a slow grin spread across his face. "I think so, too."

"Do you still want me to stay?" I asked, afraid he'd say no, afraid he'd say yes.

He bit his bottom lip nervously, but gave me a nod. His eyes closed, and he whispered, "I want you to stay in my bed."

I couldn't hide my surprise at his blatant request; I gasped, and my body froze. He was quick to respond. "No, not for sex," he blurted out. "I just want... I don't know, I just..." he shook his head.

"You just want someone to hold you," I finished for him. "You need to feel connected?" He'd been so *disconnected* from other people for far too long.

He looked at me with widened, scared eyes, and he nodded. So I kissed him. I held his jaw and pressed my mouth to his. I moved my lips against his, though not moving to deepen the kiss. When I pulled away, I stood up and offered him my hand.

He took my hand and led me to his bedroom. We undressed to our underwear and tee-shirts in silence, and I could tell he was nervous. So I pulled back the covers and slid into his bed. "Not for sex, right?" I asked with a smile.

He smirked. "Well, we could make out a little."

I laughed, but when he slid in beside me, he burrowed into my side with his head on my chest. Yes, it was intimate, and yes, it was sweet. My arms folded around him, and we talked.

I guess some questions are best asked in the dark, because he asked me about past boyfriends, ex-lovers and first times.

I answered honestly, and he told me his. He was reserved before his parents died. His sexuality was very hidden, very denied. And then his life had been on hold for almost a year and a half.

He'd not had anyone in his life, no one to hold him, no human touch for over a year. It was no wonder he wanted me to stay - even to just hold him.

His words became a little slurred and eventually his breathing evened out. He fell asleep in my arms, and for the first time in what I'd imagined felt like forever, he slept like a baby.

CHAPTER SIX

WE'D TALKED and laughed all morning and by the time we'd arrived at Callum's Gramma's in the afternoon, neither one of us had mentioned the kisses we shared the night before. He did, however, thank me again for doing this with him.

"Callum," I replied calmly. "If you thank me again, I'll make you buy me lunch for every time you say it."

He grinned and eyed me cautiously. "Is that a challenge?"

I liked this playful side to him. "Maybe."

"Thank you, thank you, thank you, thank you, thank you," he said with a laugh as we walked toward the entrance doors to the respite center.

"That's five," I said, pretending to count on my fingers. "Is that one a week for the next five weeks or lunch every day for the next five days?"

He chuckled, but as we walked inside he quieted down, his serious mood returning. His Gramma was in the common room this time, quietly flipping through a magazine. Callum smiled at one of the staff, but sat down beside his grandmother.

And by some stroke of luck or fate, or planets aligning or whatever, I was pretty sure she was having a good day. She smiled brightly. "Hello, Sweetheart."

Callum kissed her cheek and put his hand on her arm. "Hello, Gramma."

"My, you've grown."

And the grin he gave her stole my breath. It was a full blown, happy grin, like in the photos at his apartment. His eyes darted to mine, and I could see the hope and happiness shining in his eyes.

She asked how school was going, so she wasn't really in the here and now, but at least she knew it was Callum.

Callum introduced me, so I sat down with them while they talked about things I didn't even pretend to know about. After we'd been there for about fifteen minutes, Callum took a deep breath and pulled out an envelope from his jacket pocket.

"I found some photographs," he said. He pulled out the family portrait of a very young Maria with her brothers and sisters and showed it to her.

She smiled and told us she remembered how important that day was to her mother. They wore their Sunday best, did each other's hair and shined their shoes. Callum pointed to some of her sisters and brothers and asked who they are. When he pointed to the tall, dark haired boy, she called him William.

"Though his friends called him Billy," she said wistfully. "I never much cared for that name. I thought William sounded more adult."

"Did Granddaddy Hale call him Billy?"

She smiled and answered softly. "All the time."

She looked up, and I could see she was recalling memories in her mind. "They were inseparable."

Callum nodded and pulled out the small photograph of Hale and Billy that was hidden in the watch. "Is this them?"

His grandmother looked at the photograph and was silent for a long while before she nodded. Her gnarled finger touched the two smiling faces in the photo. "They were very... *close*. Spent all their time together. Hale would come to visit; that's how I met him. I was the annoying little sister that wanted to tag along... but they would sneak off..."

"You know, I wasn't blind," she said with a shake of her head. "I saw the looks they'd give each other..." her words died away, and I thought for a moment she'd said all she wasgoing to say. But then she told us, "My father caught them. Doing what... I can only guess."

Callum's eyes widened and his mouth fell open.

His grandmother continued her story with a soft, saddened voice. "Hale tried to reason with my father, telling him he was secretly in love with me and spent time with William only to be close to me. But my father didn't believe it."

Callum whispered, "What happened?"

"Father flew into a rage. He told Hale if he was any kind of man, if it was me he was after, he should marry me at once." Then she added, "I was only seventeen."

"What happened to Billy?"

His Gramma was quiet for a long while. "Father sent him off to war," she told us. "I remember that day so clearly. Father gave William a handful of money and told him not to set foot in his house - not to come back- until he was real man."

"William left two days later. Though I did see him before he left for Fort Bliss," she added pensively. "He came to see me when our father was at work and gave me a velvet pouch to give to Hale. It was a watch..."

Callum's eyes glistened, though he didn't cry. He nodded instead.

"Hale promised to marry me to save William from a terrible beating, I'm sure," she said. "But I adored him. He kept his promise, and when I turned eighteen, we were wed."

Then she whispered, "We got news of William's death not long after." Her face clouded over. "I don't think Hale ever got over it. Despite our beginning, we were married for 56 wonderful years."

Callum slipped his hand over his Gramma's frail fingers. "My grandfather was a good man."

She smiled beautifully. "He sure was."

But she looked weary. The trip down memory lane had taken its toll. I wasn't the only one who noticed. Callum helped her back to her room, and he promised to visit her tomorrow. He held her hand until she fell asleep.

CALLUM OPENED the door to his apartment and waited for me to walk in first. I scooped up Lucy, giving her a quick scratch under the chin, and Callum smiled at me as he threw his keys on the table.

He'd been quiet since we left his Gramma and on the drive to his house. I could tell he wanted to say something, and it wasn't until we were in the privacy of his home that the flood gates finally opened.

He told me how proud he is of a man he never knew. How in awe he was of what those boys did and what they went through. What they did for love... what they sacrificed for each other. He couldn't imagine their bravery, he'd said.

He couldn't imagine their heartbreak.

And now he was torn what to do.

"What do you mean?" I asked.

"The watch," he answered. "What do I do with it?"

I wasn't sure what he meant. He continued anyway, "My grandfather wanted it buried with him. I can set that right; I can see it gets buried with him. Or..." his words trailed away.

"Or what?"

He shrugged. "Or do I keep it, so their story is never forgotten?"

I smiled at him. "Cal, you don't need to decide that today. Take some time to think about it."

He nodded. "Part of me wants to see my Grandfather's last wish come true, but part of me feels they shouldn't have to hide anymore..."

"You are a lot like your Grandfather," I told him. "You are a good man."

He smiled and looked to his feet, a mixture of shy and proud. I stood in front of him. "Cal?"

He looked at me then. His eyes were warm and honest. "That's three times you've called me that."

"Is that okay?" I asked softly.

He smiled and nodded. "I like it."

"Can I suggest something?" I asked.

He nodded.

"Write their story."

His eyes widened, his mouth opened. So I explained, "You want to write, yes?" He nodded, so I continued, "Put their story into words. That way you can bury the watch if you have to, to fulfill your grandfather's wish. Because if you write it Cal, their love can never be forgotten."

He smiled at me then; one of those steal-your-breath, double dimpled smiles. Just for me. Laughing, he threw his arms around me and nodded into my neck, "Yes, ohmygod yes. That's so perfect."

CHAPTER SEVEN

I WALKED FROM THE CAR, and when I got over the small rise, I could see him. He was standing arm in arm with my mom. He had become such an important part of my life - the center of it really – since that fateful day a year ago. The day he walked into Harper Antiquities, the day he walked into my life.

I remembered every minute. How could I ever forget? I remembered our first time making love; it was weeks after that first night I'd stayed with him. We'd been close a lot of times, but the actual act of love making was something to be savored between us, we knew it was going to be special.

And it was.

It still is. Every time.

I remembered when he asked me to move in with him; I remembered going to sleep with him, waking up next to him. I remembered our first disagreement, I remembered laughing so much our sides hurt. I remembered everything.

I watched him now, standing with my family as I walked toward him. He and my mom, in particular, had become very close. My dad, who adored him, stood on his other side. My brother and his girlfriend of eight months, Libby, stood not too far behind them.

When I got to them, Mom handed Callum over to me, and I took him into my arms and kissed the side of his head. "You ready?"

He nodded, so I handed him what I was holding; what I went back to the car to get.

A book and a small velvet pouch.

He took them in trembling hands, and I kept my arm around him.

It was a hard day. Such a hard day.

He was saying goodbye to his Gramma, his only living relative. Only she wasn't living anymore. She passed away five days ago...

We'd been at home when we got the phone call; Callum should come quick. Her dementia had steadily gotten worse, her memories jumbled and nonsensical. She hadn't been well and had taken a turn for the worst. He made it in time to say goodbye, but only just.

It was late, Mom and Dad were waiting at our place when we got back, and Cal fell into my mother's arms. He cried and cried; grateful for his Gramma's pain to be gone, but he didn't know it would hit him so hard. He was truly an orphan now, he'd said.

That's what he called himself.

An orphan.

My mom had cried with him and told him, "No." She didn't know if it meant the same, but she thought of him like a son.

He sobbed. My God, he sobbed.

That's when I picked him up and carried him to bed.

When he woke the next day, he said he knew what he had to do.

He needed to bury his grandfather's watch and a copy of his book with his grandmother. She'd make sure his grandfather got it, he said. Even in the afterlife, she'd make sure he got it. "Gramma knew how much it meant."

His book, titled 'So I'll Be With You, Always' was picked up by a small publisher and was doing quite well, even though Cal had said he didn't care if he ever sold any copies. Just as long as it was done and printed on paper, he'd be happy.

But it'd done better than he ever imagined, and to know other people were hearing his grandfather's story, seeing pictures of the watch and the photographs, gave him such joy. It gave him closure; not only with his grandfather, but with his parents as well.

So that's what he was doing; he was saying goodbye to his beloved Gramma, and giving her the watch and book to take with her.

The service was small, just us and some hospice residents and staff.

Cal placed the book and the velvet pouch on top of the coffin and quickly returned to my arms, and we watched as it was swallowed by the earth.

When it was all said and done, we went home. My family followed us; Mom prepared a lunch, telling Callum it's what families do. My family rallied around him like he was one of us. His new family.

When it was dark outside and we were finally alone, I figured it was as a good a time as any. Sitting beside Cal, I held his hand and told him I had something for him.

"I know you've given your grandfather's watch back to him," I said. "And rightfully so."

I handed him a wooden box. "I got this before, and when your Gramma passed away, I wasn't sure if I should give it to you. But the more I thought about it, the more I realized it's the perfect time."

He looked from my eyes to the box in his hand, and ever so slowly, he opened it.

He looked at the shiny pocket watch embedded in the black satin, and his eyes flashed to mine. "Alex?"

I swallowed loudly, suddenly unsure of how he'd react to this.

"I thought we could start our own story," I told him. "It's a brand new C2204 Classique watch. It has a Swiss movement, skeleton dial, 17 jewel..." I stopped giving specifications, realizing it wasn't important. So instead I told him, "It was made just last year. The year we met. I was going to get it engraved for you, but didn't know if you wanted your grandfather's inscription on your watch."

"So I'll be with you, always," Callum whispered, looking from me back to the watch. He nodded, and his eyes welled with fresh tears.

"I didn't mean to upset you," I said quietly, squeezing his hand. "I just thought maybe if we carried on the tradition, our grandkids would know how much I loved you."

His head shot up and he blinked back tears. "Grandkids?"

I smiled and shrugged. "One day... maybe... I thought-"

My words were cut off by his lips on mine. He kissed me with hard, smiling lips and tear streaked cheeks.

He pulled away, only to look at the watch in his hand once again. "So I'll be with you, always," he whispered again.

"Yes," I nodded. "So I'll be with you, always."

THE STORY OF BILLY & HALE

~THIRD PERSON POV ~

1942

"Come on," Hale laughed as he ran, leading the way. Billy followed him, grinning.

They rounded the corner into the barn; into the dark, into a stall, into each other's arms.

Away from prying eyes.

Maria, Billy's younger sister, had been called inside. Hale and Billy seized the opportunity to be alone. Finally.

"Did she follow?" Hale asks. His hands were on his lover, but his eyes were wide, hesitant until they knew for sure.

"Yes," Billy said with a smile. "Mother called her to help with supper."

Billy took Hale's hand, threading their fingers. The two men stood in silence, their chests heaving with short breaths, their eyes darkened, just staring at each other.

"Are we alone?" Hale breathed, wishing, hoping it were true.

Billy nodded, his black hair falling down his forehead. Hale stretched his free hand and softly brushed the hair from his eyes before sliding his hand along the jaw of the man in front of him.

And then he kissed him.

Softly at first, like they'd done a thousand times. Their lips parted and tongues gently caressed, making both men moan quietly.

It was forbidden.

It was wrong.

But it was so very right.

They were in love.

They'd been friends at school and kept company on weekends; their fathers worked together at the County printing press, and their mothers met weekly at church auxiliary meetings.

So when the boys befriended each other, studied together, ran track together, swam together, no one suspected a thing.

No one in their right mind would suspect them to be lovers.

According to the town folk, homosexuals were strange men living in big cities; not young men from a small town who did their chores before school, who smiled politely, who opened doors for ladies.

They'd fought it at first.

Father Tom had taught them, and every kid in the parish, it was not God's will for men to love other men.

But the boys had gotten close. As the boys had become men, the tension between them grew; there were lingering looks, innocent touches.

And when they'd been talking about which girl they would ask to the senior dance, they both smiled and joked about which girls they liked.

They both knew they were lying.

They knew each other too well.

So standing a little too close, Hale swallowed his fear and asked Billy if it was really a girl he was interested in. Billy had to only shake his head, just a little; that was all it took.

Neither one of them breathed.

They just stared.

Wide eyed and petrified, Hale skimmed Billy's fingers with his own and nodded.

That was all.

That was all it took.

Billy ran all the way home from Hale's house. He didn't stop once. But he paced and paced in the privacy of his room, trying to tamper the nausea, the exhilaration, the butterflies he felt and not knowing what to do.

But he did know.

He'd known for a while.

Hale wasn't just his best friend.

He dreamed of him. In ways that men shouldn't.

And Hale had all but admitted he felt the same.

So under the cover of darkness, Billy snuck into Hale's room like he'd done a hundred times.

Only this time, they didn't trade baseball cards or talk of the war. They sat in silence.

And held hands.

Three days later, they were roughhousing in the water at the river, tackling and splashing like they always did. When Hale had grabbed his friend, a laughing Billy slipped from his grasp, and without thinking, he turned quickly and kissed his friend.

Both men stopped dead; hearts pounding, chests heaving.

And they kissed again. And again. Frenching, Billy had called it, making the blond man blush. Billy gasped when Hale's cheeks tinted red and skimmed his fingers along his cheek. And then he kissed him again.

They'd talked about the Bible, what Father Tom had taught them. And they talked of how it scared them. And they talked of their fathers who would skin them both alive if they ever found out.

That's what scared them the most.

Out of fear, they agreed to not let it happen again.

But the tension between them became too much; the looks of longing, the extended silences, the air was static.

And Billy couldn't take it.

He told Hale if he was doomed to an eternity in Hell, it didn't matter. "It couldn't be any worse than what I'm going through now," he'd said.

"Knowing how you feel in my arms, how you taste on my lips," he whispered, "it kills me to think I'll never know it again."

Hale didn't respond with words. He threw his arms around him and kissed him; open mouths, exploring tongues. The men fell against Hale's single bed, their fully clothed bodies aligning perfectly. And soon both men were wracked with waves of pleasure.

Six months on and the young men were yet to consummate their relationship with the act of lovemaking. They had explored each other's bodies, bringing the other to climax many times; always quietly, hidden. Secret and forbidden.

They made plans to go to California to college so they could be together and make love for the first time. Away from God-fearing priests, fierce fathers and annoying little sisters; where they wouldn't have to hide in a barn.

Hale had lost count of the times they'd fooled around in the barn. He'd forever link the scent of fresh-cut hay to the black-haired boy with smiling blue eyes and soft lips.

In hindsight, Hale should have known better.

The afternoon was getting on, Maria had been called inside to help Mrs. James with supper. He should have known Mr. James would be home soon.

But he was too preoccupied with Billy to hear the automobile come down the drive. In that moment, all he knew was the way Billy's hands skimmed under his shirt, over his chest, his back.

He was too distracted by whispered words of love and gentle tongues to hear footsteps or to hear the horses unsettle.

By then it was too late.

When Mr. James threw the stall door open, the boys flew apart, even though it was too apparent to Billy's father what he'd just interrupted.

Shirts untucked, unbuttoned pants, swollen lips, tousled hair.

The older man froze; his face drained of color, then of emotion.

It took a moment for Hale to realize Billy's father was telling the boys to pray for their souls, whispered with an eerie calm.

It wasn't the stone cold whisper of Mr. James' words that scared Hale.

It was the look in his eyes.

Billy saw it too. That glazed, wild look his father would

get in his eyes; the same look he'd have when breaking Mr. Colin's wild horses.

But when both boys didn't move – couldn't move – Mr. James' wrath took flight.

He yelled and screamed at them; the abomination, the disgrace, the immorality. *How would God make them suffer?* He screamed at them. He towered over the young men, who were still too terrified to move, demanding to know what punishment would fit *this* crime?

By this time, Mrs. James and Maria had to run to the barn to see what the commotion was about. They ran into the barn just in time to see Mr. James rip his stockwhip off the wall and swing it at his son.

Billy never flinched. He knew it was coming. He knew this was it.

And in a moment – a split second – Hale saw the defeated look on Billy's face; the same look the freshly broken horses would have after Mr. James has whipped them until they could barely walk.

And without thinking of his own safety, Hale stepped in between them with his arms raised up. "I can explain!" he cried. "Mr. James, please. Sir, let me explain."

Mr. James let the whip fall, though he glared wildly at the boy who would dare be brave enough to stop him.

Mr. James pointed the handle of the whip at Hale. "Out of respect for your father, I will give you ten seconds."

"Billy and I-"

"WILLIAM!" the older man yelled, making Hale jump.

"Yes, Sir. William and I were mucking out the stables, Sir. I flicked soiled hay at him and we wrestled," Hale lied for all he was worth. He looked Billy's father in the eye. "It was my fault, Sir. I started it."

Mr. James stared at Hale. And as scared as he was, as

truly frightened as he was, he never blinked.

Mr. James looked at Billy with pure disdain. "Is that what happened, William?"

Billy nodded and whispered, "Yes, Sir."

Mr. James seemed to calm a fraction; the wild look in his eyes now a hardened glare. Hale wasn't sure if Billy's father truly believed him, or if he'd rather believe the lie than consider the alternative.

The older man looked between the two. "Prove it."

Billy looked at his father, confused by his request. "Prove what, Sir?"

Mr. James' anger resurged and he took a menacing step toward his son. "Prove to me you're a man!"

Movement at the door caught Hale's eye; the two women at the door huddled together, frightened at the scene before them. And he said the first thing that came to him. "I'm in love with Maria."

All eyes turned to him; Billy's even wider than Maria's. Hale looked at Mr. James and quickly went on to say, "It's true. We've spent a lot of time together over the summer. Maria has been with us almost every day." Hale's eyes darted back to the younger sister of the man he loved. "She's a remarkable young woman."

Mr. James turned and gruffly addressed his daughter. "Is this true?"

And Maria smiled. She'd been the younger, annoying sister they'd spent most of the summer trying to ditch so they could spend time together. And Hale knew how the young girl looked at him; he wasn't blind.

Yet he couldn't bring himself to be sorry. Hale had no doubt – none whatsoever – that this lie saved Billy's life.

"Yes Father, it's true," Maria told him.

Mr. James looked at Hale. "You would marry Maria?"

Without hesitation, to prove his love for Billy, Hale nodded. "Yes, Sir."

And Billy was certain, that if his heart wasn't hammering so hard in his chest, it would have surely broken, right then and there.

Mr. James turned again to face his son. He stared at him for a long moment with such contempt, such disregard, taking pleasure in the boy's misery. Then he took his wallet out of his coat pocket and handed Billy a handful of notes.

"There's a deployment drive for Fort Bliss in town. You will sign up tomorrow, and you will be on that bus that leaves in two days," he ordered coldly. He walked toward the barn door and stopped. He didn't turn around, he just simply said, "You can sleep in the barn. You're not to step a foot inside my house until you come back a man."

Mr. James then looked at Hale. "I'll speak to you inside. You will organize a formal engagement to my daughter. We'll see if you're a *man* of your word."

With a brief glance at Billy, Hale followed Mr. James into the house, where it was arranged that a proper dinner would be held for the James' and the Winters' to discuss the upcoming marriage.

When Hale left, it was dark. But he didn't bother sneaking in to check on Billy in the barn; he knew he wouldn't be there.

And when he slipped into his upstairs room, Billy was there waiting in the dark. This time when they lay together with clinging hands and digging fingers, instead of hushed cries of pleasure, it was with quiet sobs and silent tears.

When Hale woke, his head was throbbing, his was heart

aching, and he was alone.

Billy had woken sometime during the night and with a whispered goodbye and a lingering kiss to his love's sleeping lips, he left.

Hale moved through the morning, expecting someone to jostle him, waking him from this nightmare.

Of course no one did.

It only reinforced the heavy, hollow ache in his chest when his mother insisted they visit the James' house. Celebrations were in order, Hale's mother had declared, and afternoon tea would be served.

When they arrived at the James' house, dressed in their Sunday best, Maria slipped her hand into Hale's.

She smiled sweetly, dreamily, as their mothers discussed weddings and dresses and invitations and guest lists and how the church gardens would be in flower in Spring, after Maria had come of age.

As the women talked, Hale kept expecting Billy to bound down the stairs, his laughter following close behind him. But of course, he never did.

Wondering where Billy was, what he was doing, Hale sat in a daze of sorrow and regret, numb to the world around him. Only when his own mother had asked, "Where's young William?" did a silence fall over them.

Hale's heart had clenched woefully before dropping to his feet. He almost gasped at the pain of it. But Maria had squeezed his hand in hers, holding on tightly – and he knew then he had an ally in Billy's sister.

She smiled at him, though he could see the hurt in her eyes. And he understood he and this girl, soon to be his wife, both loved the same man.

Mrs. James explained quietly that her eldest son was going to war.

Hale didn't hear the talk of the First Armored Division or training at Fort Knox or expected deployments to North Africa. He heard none of it.

He heard his heart re-break in his chest a thousand times over. He heard silence where there should have been laughter. He felt a small, soft hand in his when it should have been bigger, harder. He smelt perfumes and powders when it should have been musk and sweat.

When they returned home, Hale had declared himself tired and not hungry, and had retired to his room. The sky outside darkened as he lay on his bed staring at the ceiling. He wondered where Billy was, unable to go home. He wondered how on Earth his life had gone from perfect just the day before to now be so horribly wrong.

And after 10 PM under the cover of darkness like he'd done so many times before, Billy climbed up to Hale's window.

Billy threw his satchel in before him, making Hale leap to the window. He grabbed Billy and all but pulled him through, not even giving him time to stand before he had his arms around him.

Hale fired question after question; where had he been, he'd been so worried, where did he go early this morning, why did he leave without saying goodbye, didn't he realize how much he loved him?

Billy kissed him quiet, the questions – and answers – soon forgotten. Unable to get enough of each other, they kissed deeply, holding on as tight as they dared.

When they pulled their mouths away to breathe, Hale pulled Billy onto his bed, and onto his lap.

He held him, cradled him, running his hands over every part he could reach. He buried his face into his neck, inhaling his scent deeply, willing himself to never forget it.

Billy curled himself around the man he loved, his legs straddling him, his arms holding him close. Hale's fingers caged Billy's face, and he pulled back, only to stare at him trying to memorize his features, his eyes scanning every inch of his face.

"Run away with me," Hale whispered, the idea coming to him in a flash. "We'll leave tonight. Just you and me."

Billy smiled sadly, and his eyes slowly closed. "I can't."

"Why not?" Hale disputed.

"I'm already enrolled," Billy whispered. "My father saw to it this morning."

"It doesn't matter," Hale tried to reason, unable to hide the desperation from his voice. "They won't find us."

Billy's silence was his answer; the tortured look in his eyes. The haunted sadness he saw there told Hale this argument was over.

"I can't run from the Army," Billy finally said, defeated.

"Why is he doing this?" Hale asked. Billy knew he was asking about his father.

"He wants to separate us, any way he can. He's proving a point," Billy admitted quietly. Then he added, "Because he's a cruel man."

"I hate him," Hale hissed. "He's marrying his daughter off; not for her happiness, but so he can see me suffer every day. And he'd rather send you off to war..." he groaned; a tortured sound. "...if anything were to happen to you..."

Billy swallowed thickly, his blue eyes slowly closed. "So you're marrying Maria?"

Tears welled in Hale's eyes and spilled slowly down his cheeks. "I didn't have a choice, Billy," he said, his voice broke with emotion. "He would have killed you. I've seen that look on his face before when he's taken whips and sticks to horses. I couldn't let him do that to you."

Billy put his fingers against Hale's lips. "Shhh," he whispered; then he wiped the tears from his cheeks with his thumbs.

"I love you," Billy whispered. "I will love you, always."

"Always," Hale breathed.

Billy kissed him and whispered against his lips, "I want you to make love to me."

Hale's eyes widened and his breath caught in his throat. But Billy leaned in and whispered in Hale's ear, "I want this with you before I go. I want to feel you inside me. Just this once."

Hale pulled Billy's face back to see him clearly. Billy shifted in Hale's lap so he was pressing harder against him. He looked Hale in the eye so he couldn't doubt his conviction.

"If this is all I have, I want it with you," Billy told him as tears filled his eyes. "No one can take this away from us."

Hale kissed him then, deeply, urgently - suddenly aware of how little time they had. He pushed Billy backward so he was laying on top of him, settling between his legs, their mouths open and fused.

They'd talked about this. They knew the mechanics of it, and as scary as it was, it felt right. This was going to happen; he was about to lose his virginity... to a man.

Not just any man, but to a man he loved.

Billy.

Hale moaned, kissing down his jaw, his neck.

"Hale," Billy's hushed voice whispered warm against his neck. "My bag. Get my bag."

It took a moment for Hale to reconcile Billy's words with actions – and ignoring his aching groin, he shook his head and retrieved Billy's bag from the floor.

Billy chuckled quietly at him, but rifling through the

small knapsack, pulled out a small white bottle and a cardboard packet.

Hale's eyes flew to Billy's, and all the dark haired boy could do was bite his lip and explain, "I got these today. I went to Smithfield and found a drug store."

"You did?" Hale asked quietly. "You planned this?"

Billy nodded. "Last night when we laid here... well, I realized this might be it for us. It's all I could think about." Then he leaned up and kissed Hale's lips. "I want this memory of us."

Hale took the condoms and lubrication jelly with shaking hands. "I don't want to hurt you."

"You won't," Billy whispered fervently. "You could never hurt me."

Hale searched his eyes for a flicker of doubt. "Are you sure?"

Billy answered by sliding his hand around Hale's neck and pulling him down, so he laid over him once more and kissed him.

Billy had never kissed Hale like that before; it was pleading and serious. It was consuming and it was now, or never.

And Hale knew this was it.

He undressed his lover slowly, relishing in every reveal of skin, every brush of naked bodies. It was the first time both men had been fully naked in bed, and Hale savored every inch of the body laid out before him.

He took him into his mouth and pressed his fingers against the tight opening where he would soon lose himself. He pushed inside with his fingers and tongued the rigid length until Billy was writhing, bucking and begging.

Hale looked up to find Billy's hands fisted into the

sheets beside them, his head pushed back into the pillows, his chest arched off the bed as he worked him over.

And when Hale felt Billy buck and flex underneath him, when he felt the cock in his mouth and hand swell and jerk, he didn't pull away.

No, he sucked harder and drank every pulsing drop.

He wanted to taste him.

He needed to know.

And with shaking hands, he clumsily rolled the condom down his own aching erection and applied the jelly. Falling forward onto his hands, his face level with Billy's, he kissed him.

The dark haired man moaned, drunk on his orgasm high, his eyes barely open. And when Hale pushed the blunt head of his cock against his opening, Billy's eyes widened.

Hale looked for doubt, for fear, but found none. Only love and insistence so he slipped forward, slowly, surely.

Billy gasped, and Hale froze. But Billy whispered, "Keep going," and wrapped his arms around him to keep him in place. He pulled his knees up so Hale could enter him easier.

And when Hale could go no deeper, he pulled back only to rock back inside him again. He kissed his lover's lips, and they stole each other's breaths.

Knowing he was nearing his release, Hale murmured, "It's too much."

Billy nodded and gasped as Hale thrust into him, "It's everything."

Hale could only nod, trying to control his breathing, his body. Billy knew Hale was close to finishing by the way his body trembled, by the look in his eyes. He cupped his face with his hands, and told him, "I'll remember this, always."

And with a strangled sob, he thrust in sharply once more, filling the condom inside his lover. There were no words to describe the pleasure. There were no words to describe the love.

And Billy held him as he cried.

He wrapped his arms around him. And in a mass of tangled arms and legs in that small single bed, the two men didn't sleep.

They whispered words of love and regret with kisses to lips and necks. And when desire grew to be too much, this time it was Billy who took charge. He lay over Hale, holding him, adoring him and eased inside of him.

Hale yearned for the pain and the stretch of his lover claiming him; a token reminder of what they'd shared. He savored the feel of Billy inside him, this first time.

This last time.

And before the sun rose, they didn't dare say the word; though they knew what it was.

Goodbye.

Instead Billy smiled, holding Hale's face as he kissed him one last time and disappeared out the window.

Hale stared at where Billy had once stood. He marveled at how the human heart kept beating, even though it was surely broken. His lungs still took air, even though they burned. He wondered how the world still turned, when in fact, his world had just stood still.

Yet the sun still shone, life went on.

And while Hale sat on his bed, trying to find the will to even stand, Billy was running one last errand.

He had one more job to do.

And by the time the town had gathered along Main Street to bid the bus of brave young men goodbye, it was done.

Under the watchful, spiteful eye of his father, Billy kissed his mother goodbye, his younger siblings too, and he hugged Maria hard. "Remember what I told you," he whispered.

"Yes, William," she'd nodded.

"Look after him," he murmured.

Hale stood at the back of the crowd, not wanting to see him leave, but unable to stay away. Only when he saw the striking man in his army greens, his feet pulled him forward.

If Maria hadn't stopped him, he would have walked right up to him and threw his arms around him. She took his arm and pulled him close, whispering in Hale's ear. "Don't give him a reason to kill you," she whispered, giving a pointed nod toward her father. "He's come to see to it. That you two are done."

Hale stopped. He knew Maria was right. But despite the movement around them, the two men stood and stared as people passed between them.

Maria leaned in and whispered, while neither man looked away, "William gave me something to give to you." And with the jostling of the crowd, Mr. James didn't see Maria slip a velvet pouch into Hale's hand. But Billy did.

Hale quickly looked down at the gift before his eyes darted back to Billy's, and he nodded. Hale slipped the pouch into his breast pocket and only when the sergeant yelled roll call, did Billy turn away.

Hale watched him climb the steps on the bus, taking a seat, and their eyes met again.

Hale wanted to move, he wanted to get Billy off that bus. He wanted to do something... anything. But he couldn't. He couldn't move. His life was ending right before him and he was powerless to stop it.

And as the bus pulled away, Billy mouthed just one

word. Just for him.

Always.

Hale had thought the day Billy left would be the hardest day of his life.

Oh, how wrong he'd been.

It was a sunny day, he and Maria were at home; Maria had brought out lemonade while Hale tended to the yard when old Mr. Bancroft had called in. Not seeing Hale in the garden, he walked to the front door.

Hale could just make out what the man said. "You'd best go and see your mother."

And then he took off his hat.

Maria came running, leaving the old man at the door, and it was the look in her eyes. Fear.Loss.

And Hale knew.

He just knew.

She took Hale's hand, and they ran the two blocks to her parent's house where the hardest day of Hale's life took hold.

Mr. James stood at the kitchen counter, stoic, resigned. Mrs. James was crying as she was uselessly thumping at her husband's chest with her small fists, clutching a yellow piece of paper.

"You sent him away," she sobbed. "You killed my son." Mr. James just stood there. He didn't move. He didn't speak.

Maria ran to her mother, pulling her away from her father; the yellow note fell from her hand and feathered to the floor.

And Hale knew what it meant.

He didn't have to read it.

He knew when Mrs. Dwyer from down the road was handed a yellow envelope what it told her.

That her boy wasn't coming home.

Hale knew from the paper on the floor.

Billy wasn't coming home.

Maria took her mother out and up the stairs, leaving Hale alone with Mr. James.

Hale bent over and picked the piece of paper up from the floor. He saw *The United States Army...* and he didn't read any more.

He didn't have to.

Placing it face down on the table, he turned to Maria's father. Hale's voice was quiet, detached. "When you go to church on Sunday, tell me, will it be Billy's soul you pray for, or your own?"

He didn't give the older man time answer.

Hale stared at the man he despised. "Or will you ask for forgiveness?" He took a step toward him, and Mr. James flinched. "Because I assure you, you won't *ever* be forgiven. Not by me, not by Maria, not by your wife." Hale's voice shook. "And not by God."

"I'm not a sinner," Mr. James said weakly, his voice cracking.

"Yes, you are," Hale breathed. "You're a murderer."

Mr. James looked at him then, but Hale continued quietly, pointing his finger at his chest. "And if I'm going to Hell for *loving* him, then I will damn well see you there."

"Hale?" Maria's quiet voice called from the door. "Is everything alright?"

He turned to face his young wife, and seeing her unshed tears, he quickly crossed the small room to hold her. "Momma's resting," she sobbed quietly in his arms. "William... William's..."

"Shhh," he hushed her. "Don't say it. Please don't say it." Hale looked over the top of Maria's head and stared at her father. And he silently dared the old man to say something, to open his sorry mouth and make just one comment, and Hale would have gladly torn him to pieces.

But he never did.

Mr. James hardly spoke a word again. Not to anyone.

His guilt kept company with his liquor; poisonous and ever present.

A part of Hale died that day. He felt it. The discernible snap of his heart breaking, dying, right there in his chest. Never to be whole again.

Maria nursed both her mother and Hale through their broken hearts, including her own. And it was then Hale really saw the woman he married for what she was, for who she was.

She was strong and resilient. And Hale came to realize she was funny, adoring, smart... and beautiful.

Hale still saw Billy in his wife, the eyes, the smile.

But he saw Maria too.

She was a good woman. She was kind and patient. And she knew.

She knew, and she loved him anyway.

And seeing her laugh would make him smile.

They'd tried for a long time to fall pregnant. The doctors had said Maria's body was not compatible with conceiving. And when by the grace of God they did conceive a son, the birth nearly killed them both.

That was when Hale realized he loved Maria. He loved her, like he had loved Billy.

The nurse had come to get him, telling him there'd been complications, and he should prepare himself for grief.

That was when he realized just how much he loved her.

When she was almost taken from him too, it made him realize. God, how he *loved* her. He realized then she's been the one who kept him together these past years and just how wrong it had been.

He promised to God if He spared Maria's life, he'd take better care of her. He'd treat her how she deserved to be treated. He'd be the husband she deserved, because he loved her.

And the doctors said both mother and child would be okay.

They had talked of names for the child before and decided if it were a boy, they would call him William. But when Hale saw his son for the first time with his fair hair instead of Billy and Maria's black, and with his promise to God fresh in his mind, he suggested they call him Peter.

"Peter?" Maria asked.

Hale nodded, and with a quiet voice, he told her he was sorry. He never meant to bring Billy into their marriage, into their lives as a husband and wife. And he didn't think it was right if their son was brought into the world in the shadow of another man.

"Billy's gone. I know that now," Hale said. "But you and Peter are here. You are a gift to me. And I love you, Maria Winters."

On the day Peter was christened, Hale sat on his bed and held the only two mementos he had of Billy; the small photograph of the two of them--the photo his own Maria had taken--and the pocket watch. He looked at the photo one last time, at Billy's smiling face, slipped it in the back of the watch and put them away.

Maria sat down beside him and held his hand. He smiled and kissed her lips. "I'll take it with me when I'm dead and gone, but for as long as there's breath in me, I'm yours."

Over the next fifty years, Hale could count on one hand the times he took out the watch. He kept his word to his Maria.

He spent fifty years with this woman. He adored her.

And at the end of their fifty years, he didn't need any doctors to tell him his blood wasn't right – he knew he wasn't well.

As his body gave out, he held Maria's hand, closed his eyes and said his final goodbyes.

Only when he opened his eyes again, it wasn't Maria he saw.

It was a tall, black haired boy with dark eyes and half a smirk, wearing Army greens.

"I've waited a long time for you," he said with a blinding smile.

"How could you find me?" Hale asked, patting down his pockets. "I don't have the watch."

Billy threw his head back and laughed; the sound of bells rang sweet in the air. "You silly boy. I didn't need the watch to find you."

"My grandson will need it, won't he?" Hale asked. He didn't know *how* he knew; he just *knew*. "Callum, Peter's son. He's going to need the watch."

Billy nodded. "Yes. He'll need it to find what he's looking for."

With the smile of an angel, Billy took Hale's hand and led him toward the light.

The End

ABOUT THE AUTHOR

N.R. Walker is an Australian author, who loves her genre of gay romance.
She loves writing and spends far too much time doing it, but wouldn't have it any other way.

She is many things; a mother, a wife, a sister, a writer. She has pretty, pretty boys who live in her head, who don't let her sleep at night unless she gives them life with words.

She likes it when they do dirty, dirty things...but likes it even more when they fall in love.

She used to think having people in her head talking to her was weird, until one day she happened across other writers who told her it was normal.

She's been writing ever since...

The Weight Of It All

Switched

Point of No Return

Breaking Point

Starting Point

Spencer Cohen Book One

Spencer Cohen Book Two

Spencer Cohen Book Three

Yanni's Story

On Davis Row

Free Reads:

Sixty Five Hours

Learning to Feel

His Grandfather's Watch (And The Story of Billy and Hale)

The Twelfth of Never (Blind Faith 3.5)

Twelve Days of Christmas (Sixty Five Hours Christmas)

Best of Both Worlds

Translated Titles:

Fiducia Cieca (Italian translation of Blind Faith)

Attraverso Questi Occhi (Italian translation of Through These Eyes)

Preso alla Sprovvista (Italian translation of Blindside)

Il giorno del Mai (Italian translation of Blind Faith 3.5)

Cuore di Terra Rossa (Italian translation of Red Dirt Heart)

Cuore di Terra Rossa 2 (Italian translation of Red Dirt Heart 2)

Cuore di Terra Rossa 3 (Italian translation of Red Dirt Heart 3)

Cuore di Terra Rossa 4 (Italian translation of Red Dirt Heart 4)

Intervento di Retrofit (Italian translation of Elements of Retrofit)

Confiance Aveugle (French translation of Blind Faith)

A travers ces yeux: Confiance Aveugle 2 (French translation of Through These Eyes)

Aveugle: Confiance Aveugle 3 (French translation of Blindside)

À Jamais (French translation of Blind Faith 3.5)

Cronin's Key (French translation)

Cronin's Key II (French translation)

Au Coeur de Sutton Station (French translation of Red Dirt Heart)

Partir ou rester (French translation of Red Dirt Heart 2)

Faire Face (French translation of Red Dirt Heart 3)

Trouver sa Place (French translation of Red Dirt Heart 4)

Rote Erde (German translation of Red Dirt Heart)

Rote Erde 2 (German translation of Red Dirt Heart 2)